MW01047102

THALIA BROWN AND THE BLUE BUG

MICHELLE DIONETTI
Illustrated by JAMES CALVIN

THALIA BROWN
AND THE
BLUE BUG

Addison-Wesley ▲▼

Text Copyright © 1979 by Michelle Dionetti
Illustrations Copyright © 1979 by James Calvin
All Rights Reserved
Addison-Wesley Publishing Company, Inc.
Reading, Massachusetts 01867
Printed in the United States of America
ABCDEFGHIJK-WZ-79

Book Designed by Charles Mikolaycak

Library of Congress Cataloging in Publication Data
Dionetti, Michelle, 1947—
    Thalia Brown and the blue bug.

    SUMMARY: Feeling neglected by her family, Thalia
Brown finds someone else to help her get ready for the
Art Fair.
    [1. Family life — Fiction] I. Calvin, James.
II. Title.
PZ7.D6214Th   [Fic]   79-4160
ISBN 0-201-01399-1

For Nina, Christian, and Aaron

GRANMA BROWN HOLDS THE BABY. HE IS small and brown against her big white jacket. Daddy Brown talks to James. Their heads are close together. They are talking low, to each other.

"Hey, Daddy!" says Thalia Brown.

She pulls at Daddy's arm. Daddy keeps on talking to James. Thalia sticks her head underneath Daddy's elbow.

"Hey, Daddy," she says. "What're you doing?"

"We're busy, Thalia," says James. "Go away."

Thalia Brown sticks her tongue out at James.

"Thalia," says Daddy, "James and I are talking now. Please stop pestering."

Thalia Brown goes to Granma. She leans against Granma's soft arm. Granma sings to the baby in a quiet voice. He is almost asleep. Thalia Brown touches his head. She likes the way his hair feels.

"Keep your hands to yourself, Thalia!" says Granma Brown.

Thalia Brown goes outside. She sits on the cement of the small yard in back of her building. She sits under Miss Washington's laundry — right under Miss Washington's nightgown.

The cement is still cool from the night. Soon it will be too hot to sit on. Thalia Brown runs her fingertips over the rough cement. It feels like sandpaper, like brick. There is a crack in the cement. There is dry dirt in the crack and some stiff blades of grass, trying to grow in the city.

Near her foot Thalia sees something blue. She picks it up. The blue comes off on her fingers. It is a piece of chalk. Thalia rubs it against the cement.

The chalk makes a powdery uneven line. It does not go exactly where Thalia Brown wants it to go. There are too many cracks in the cement. Thalia tries to color in a solid shape. No matter how hard she tries, there are still spaces.

Thalia Brown stands up to look at her piece of blue. When she stands the cracks don't show so much. The shape looks like a blue bug. All it needs is legs. Thalia draws the legs.

Thalia Brown stares at the blue bug so long it looks like it's moving. She can see the bug's house. Thalia draws the house with her blue chalk.

Thalia Brown starts to write her name on the cement. The chalk is very small from so much drawing. Just when Thalia makes the H after the T the blue chalk crumbles away. Thalia looks for something else to write with.

There is a piece of brick on the cement. Thalia Brown scratches the cement with the brick. The brick leaves a thin white line. It is not as good as the chalk for drawing, but it is better than nothing.

It begins to rain. Thalia feels one drop on her hand and another on her back. She sees round dark spots on the cement, one spot, then two. A raindrop falls on the blue bug. The light blue of the chalk turns wet, like blue mud.

The sky opens. All the water in the sky falls down, straight down, and bounces off the alley, off the cement. Thalia Brown runs up the gray wooden stairs to the back porch. She stares out at the rain.

"Hey, rain!" she yells. "You leave my bug alone!"

The rain tap-dances on the cement. It turns into a puddle at the gate. It washes the blue bug. It washes the blue bug's house. The blue bug melts into small, faint blue streams.

The back door on the second floor creaks open and slams against the side of the building. Miss Washington rushes down the stairs, one arm flung over her head to keep off the rain.

"My laundry!" she cries.

Miss Washington's clothes are limp. Water drips off them onto the cement, onto Thalia Brown's blue bug.

"My bug," says Thalia Brown.

Miss Washington and Thalia Brown stare at the rain and at the laundry and the blue bug.

"Too bad," says Miss Washington.

"Too bad," says Thalia Brown.

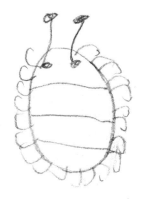

IT STOPS RAINING. THALIA BROWN comes outside. She runs down the wooden steps to the cement. Miss Washington's nightgown is still dripping on the blue bug. The blue bug isn't really a blue bug anymore. It is a blue smear. Already the sun is drying the cement around it.

Granma Brown swings open the screen door.

"Hey, Granma!" calls Thalia Brown. "That mean old rain washed away my blue bug!"

"What bug?" says Granma.

"Bug I drew on the cement," says Thalia Brown.

"Oh," says Granma. "Come here."

She hands Thalia four shiny quarters. They clink in Thalia Brown's palm.

"Go get me some raisins," says Granma.

"Okay," says Thalia Brown.

Thalia Brown likes to go to the store. She skips across the cement in back of her building.

She steps around a thousand little pieces of shiny green glass. She splashes in a puddle. Her feet make prints on the broken pavement of the alley. Thalia Brown looks over her shoulder so she can see her own footprints.

The grocery store is dark. It smells like soap. Thalia Brown finds the raisins. She stands in line behind an old man with white hair.

There are signs on the wall near the door. Thalia Brown looks at them while she waits. There is one big sign with bright red letters. It says,

```
ART FAIR
CHILDREN
BRING YOUR PICTURES
TO FIRST STREET CHURCH
SATURDAY
```

Thalia Brown smiles widely. She can draw a picture and bring it to the Art Fair! Thalia Brown can't wait to get home.

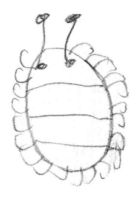

THALIA BROWN RUNS UP THE BACK porch steps and into the kitchen. The screen door slams behind her.

"Granma!" cries Thalia Brown. "I'm going to be in an Art Fair! I need some paper, Granma!"

"Hush, girl!" says Granma Brown. "You'll wake the baby!"

Granma takes the raisins and change from Thalia's hands. She puts the raisins on the table and drops the change into the coffee can next to the sink. The coins clunk! loud.

Thalia Brown stands still. She bites her lip. She wants to ask Granma for paper again, but decides she'd better not. Granma Brown walks away from her. Thalia waits until Granma is gone. Then she creeps into the bedroom.

James keeps some crayons in a shoebox under the bed. Thalia slides out the shoebox, slowly, slowly. She does not want to wake the baby. She runs her hands through the crayons,

thrum, thrum. The baby stirs. Thalia Brown takes the whole box into the kitchen.

Thalia Brown needs a piece of paper. She looks into the pantry. There is a roll of shelf paper, only a small piece left, on the top shelf.

Thalia Brown steps onto the bottom shelf next to the can of peas. She reaches up and grabs the shelf paper. Quickly she pulls the last piece of paper off the roll. It is not very big and one side is crooked. Thalia Brown folds the crooked side to make it even.

Thalia Brown draws a blue bug with a blue crayon. She colors in the bug thick and smooth.

She draws the bug's house. She draws a blue leaf for the blue bug to eat. She signs her name, T, h, a, l, i, a, B, r. She has to put o, w, n sideways in the corner because there is no more room after the r.

James comes into the kitchen.

"What're you doing with those crayons!" he says. He snatches the box.

"I just used a blue one, James," says Thalia Brown. "See?"

She holds up her picture.

"Didn't ask me first," says James.

"Can I please use a red one, James? I want to draw another bug on here."

"No!" says James.

"Why not?"

"Cause you're always grabbing my stuff," says James. "You never ask me." He takes the crayons out of the kitchen.

"You never use them, James!" cries Thalia Brown. She runs after him.

"You big ugly meanie!" she yells.

In the bedroom the baby starts to cry.

"See what you did?" yells James. "You woke him up!"

"Huh, you did!" yells Thalia Brown.

"Thalia Brown!" says Granma. She stands in the hallway. She looks very stern. "You go quiet that baby down."

Thalia Brown goes into the bedroom. Baby is standing in his crib, crying with his mouth open. Thalia Brown hugs him over the crib rails.

"It's okay, Baby," says Thalia Brown. "James is just being mean."

Baby lies down and Thalia covers him with his blanket.

"Go to sleep," she coos softly, rubbing circles on his back. "Go to sleep."

Baby closes his eyes. Thalia Brown tiptoes out of the bedroom. She goes back to the kitchen to look at her drawing. The paper is gone!

"Granma," says Thalia Brown. "Have you seen my picture of the blue bug?"

"Oh," says Granma. "You want to keep that? Thought it was trash."

She pulls a crumpled paper from the garbage pail.

Thalia Brown smooths out the paper. It will not stay flat. There is a grease spot right in the middle, right on one of the blue bug's legs.

Thalia Brown's eyes spill over. She runs out the back door and down the gray wooden stairs to the cement. She sits under Miss Washington's nightgown. She stares at the blue smear that used to be the blue bug, and she cries as hard as the rain.

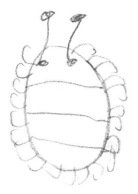

MISS WASHINGTON COMES DOWN THE stairs to get her clothes off the line. She pulls down a towel. The nightgown dips with the pulled line and bounces on Thalia Brown's head. Miss Washington pulls down a shirt. The nightgown dips again. Miss Washington comes to pull down the nightgown. She bumps into Thalia Brown's foot.

"What's that?" says Miss Washington.

She bends over and sees Thalia Brown.

"Thalia Brown!" she says. "What're you doing under there crying like the rain?"

Thalia Brown tells Miss Washington everything. She tells her about the blue bug. She tells her about the Art Fair. She tells her about the picture Granma threw in the garbage by mistake.

"Why that's nothing but a few setbacks," says Miss Washington. "Can't let a little disappointment stop you! You come upstairs with me. I've

got some paints used to belong to Junior. Got me some paper too."

Thalia Brown jumps to her feet.

"I'll help you with the laundry, Miss Washington," she says.

Together Thalia and Miss Washington pull down the rest of the dry clothes. Miss Washington carries the bag of clothespins upstairs. Thalia Brown carries the clothesbasket. She has to go up the stairs one step at a time to keep from falling with the clean wash.

Miss Washington's apartment is shaped like Thalia Brown's. The kitchen is in the same place, and the bathroom and everything. But Miss Washington's apartment isn't the same as Thalia Brown's. Miss Washington has so much furniture it's hard to move without bumping into something. And Miss Washington has lots of lace everywhere — lace curtains, lace tablecloth, lace things on the backs of chairs.

Thalia Brown puts the clothesbasket on the lace-covered kitchen table and looks around. Miss Washington is in the front bedroom. She is talking. Thalia Brown can hear her voice but she can't hear what she's saying. In a minute Miss Washington comes out with a paintbox and a whole pad of paper.

"This here's drawing paper," she says to Thalia Brown. "You can keep it. You can keep the paints too."

Thalia Brown reaches to take the gifts. She has trouble thinking of a polite thing to say. Her mind is too busy seeing all the beautiful pictures she can make. Thalia Brown smiles widely.

"Thank you, Miss Washington," she says, hugging the paintbox.

"Welcome," says Miss Washington. "Show me what you draw when you're done."

Thalia Brown takes the paintbox and the paper into a corner of the kitchen. Then she fills a bowl with water. Then she sits down and opens the paintbox.

There is a paintbrush inside and eight colors: yellow, orange, red, green, blue, purple, brown, and black. The red is almost all gone and the black is empty, but there is a lot of blue.

Thalia Brown dips the brush in the water and swishes it around the cake of blue paint. Then she begins to paint. She paints picture after picture after picture.

Thalia Brown has been working so hard on her paintings that only now she hears James' voice.

"Time for dinner, Thalia!" it says. "I've been calling you for an hour!"

"Have not," says Thalia Brown. She keeps on painting.

"Have too," says James. He comes over to see what Thalia is doing.

"Where'd you get the paints and paper?" he asks.

"Miss Washington. You can't have them."

"Don't want them," says James.

Thalia straightens up to look at her painting. "Going to be an artist when I grow up," she says.

"Yeah?" says James. "Get ready so we can eat."

After dinner Thalia Brown shows her pictures to Daddy. He looks at them all, one at a time.

"These are good, Thalia!" he says.

"Gonna be an artist when she grows up," says James.

Granma listens while she feeds the baby.

"You say something about an art fair?" she asks.

"There's one Saturday at First Street Church," says Thalia Brown.

Granma nods. She belongs to the First Street Church.

"What picture you going to enter?" she asks.

"Haven't made it yet," says Thalia Brown. "I'll do it now."

Thalia Brown sits at the kitchen table. She opens her box of paints. James comes in, bringing his box of crayons.

"Want to use these?" he asks.

"Yes!" says Thalia Brown. She takes the box and hugs it.

"You give them back!" says James. "They're still mine!"

"I will," says Thalia Brown.

Thalia Brown draws a blue bug with one of James' crayons. She colors it in smooth and thick. Then she paints Thalia Brown drawing the blue bug. She paints in the cement and Miss Washington's nightgown. When the paint is dry she takes a black crayon and prints her name, T,h,a,l,i,a,B,r,o,w,n, small and neat in the bottom corner of the picture.

"That's not bad," says James. He leans over the back of Thalia's chair to look at her picture. "Not bad at all."

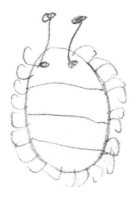

IT IS HOT ON SATURDAY MORNING THE way it always is in the city in the summer. It is hard for Thalia Brown to wait until after breakfast to bring her picture to the First Street Church.

"I'm going to show my picture to Miss Washington," she tells Granma Brown.

"You come right down here after that," says Granma. "I'm going to the Art Fair with you."

Thalia Brown doesn't say a word. She doesn't want Granma to change her mind.

Thalia runs up the back stairs to Miss Washington's. The screen door is open. Miss Washington is fixing herself breakfast.

"Morning, Thalia Brown," she says.

"Look, Miss Washington!" Thalia Brown holds her picture up for Miss Washington to see.

"Well, that's just fine!" says Miss Washington.

"Granma's going to go with me to the Art Fair!" says Thalia Brown.

"She sure must be proud of you!" says Miss Washington.

Thalia Brown skips along the sidewalk next to Granma. Granma is pushing the stroller.

"Faster, Granma!" says Thalia Brown.

"Going as fast as the old legs can," says Granma.

"I'll push the stroller," offers Thalia Brown.

"No thank you, ma'am," says Granma. "Way you're jumping you'd have that stroller going fifty miles an hour and your brother would fall right out of it."

"Oh, Granma! You worry all the time!"

"You just worry about that picture, Thalia Brown! Don't you drop it."

The First Street Church looks very festive. A big sign in front says ART FAIR. Ribbons decorate the sign. Nearby stands a wheelbarrow full of flowers. Inside more ribbons and flowers decorate two round tables. Some children's pictures are already hanging on the special display boards.

Thalia Brown shows her painting to a lady who is standing behind one of the round tables. The lady asks Thalia Brown's name and age. She asks what the title of the painting is.

Thalia Brown thinks.

" 'Thalia Brown and the Blue Bug,' "she says.

The lady writes it down on a small piece of paper. She fixes Thalia's painting to a large sheet of bright construction paper to frame it, and glues the small paper with Thalia Brown's name and age and 'Thalia Brown and the Blue Bug' to a corner of the frame. Then she hangs Thalia's picture on a display board.

Thalia Brown is proud. So is Granma. When another lady comes into the church Granma Brown nods at Thalia Brown's picture and says,

"That's my granddaughter's picture. She's going to be an artist when she grows up."

"I'm an artist now," says Thalia Brown.